Crow in the snow

Lesley Sims

Illustrated by Fred Blunt

1

Crow is flying over snow.

He spies some paw prints far below.

"Ho, ho," says Crow
and swoops down low.

"I think I'll follow where they go."

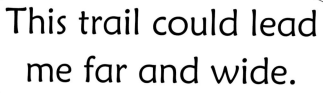

Then – five fine snowmen,
side by side.

Ho, ho!
I know...

Crow starts hopping to and fro.

He picks up sticks,
some stones and cones...

And look –
a crow made out of snow.

Crow blinks and sees the trail
goes on. "What next?" he thinks
and trots along.

He spots a red
sled by a gate,

a yellow
hat,

a fallen
skate.

The trail leads to...

...a frozen lake.

Creak!

Mice and voles
and Mole are skating.

"Oh no!" cries Crow.
"The ice is breaking."

Crack!

"Help!" calls Mole. "I'm falling in.
I'm all cold and I can't swim."

Crow flies fast.

He leaves the lake.
In seconds, he's flown past the gate.

He spies the snowmen, dives down low,
grabs a scarf and back he goes.

With one last heave, cold Mole is free.
He sits and shivers by a tree.

"Let me get the sled," says Crow...

and soon he's giving Mole a tow.

Now all are warm and safe and snug.
Mole gives a grin and lifts his mug.

"A toast," he says. "A toast to Crow. He's the hero of the snow!"

About phonics

Phonics is a method of teaching reading, used extensively in today's schools. At its heart is an emphasis on identifying the *sounds* of letters, or combinations of letters, that are then put together to make words. These sounds are known as phonemes.

Starting to read
Learning to read is an important milestone for any child. The process can begin well before children start to learn letters and put them together to read words. The sooner children can discover books and enjoy stories and language, the better they will be prepared for reading themselves, first with the help of an adult and then independently.

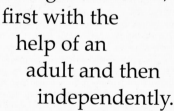

You can find out more about phonics on the Usborne Very First Reading website, **www.usborne.com/veryfirstreading** (US readers go to **www.veryfirstreading.com**). Click on the **Parents** tab at the top of the page, then scroll down and click on **About synthetic phonics.**

Phonemic awareness

An important early stage in pre-reading and early reading is developing phonemic awareness: that is, listening out for the sounds within words. Rhymes, rhyming stories and alliteration are excellent ways of encouraging phonemic awareness.

In this story, your child will soon identify the *o* sound, as in **crow** and **snow** or **stone** or **mole**. Look out, too, for rhymes such as **red** – **sled** and **gate** – **skate**.

Hearing your child read

If your child is reading a story to you, don't rush to correct mistakes, but be ready to prompt or guide if he or she is struggling. Above all, do give plenty of praise and encouragement.

Edited by Jenny Tyler
Designed by Caroline Spatz
Additional design by Sam Chandler

Reading consultants: Alison Kelly and Anne Washtell

First published in 2013 by Usborne Publishing Ltd., Usborne House, 83-85 Saffron Hill, London EC1N 8RT, England.
www.usborne.com Copyright © 2013 Usborne Publishing Ltd.

Crow in the snow

A lively story with irresistible illustrations, this book is
a delight to share with very young children. It can also be
enjoyed by children who are beginning to read for themselves.
The simple rhyming text helps to develop essential language
and early reading skills, and there are guidance notes
for parents at the back of the book.

Published in the USA by
EDC PUBLISHING
10302 E. 55th Place
Tulsa, Oklahoma 74146, USA.

Educational Development Corporation

NOT FOR SALE OUTSIDE OF THE USA

$6.99

JFMA JJASOND/16 01308/8
Printed in China.
Made with paper from a sustainable source.

For more information on Usborne books visit
www.edcpub.com or www.usbornebooksandmore.com

ISBN 978-0-7945-3141-6

9 780794 531416